X MARKS THE SPOT!

X MARKS THE SPOT!

Jeff Szpirglas & Danielle Saint-Onge
illustrated by Dave Whamond

ORCA BOOK PUBLISHERS

Library and Archives Canada Cataloguing in Publication

Szpirglas, Jeff, author
X marks the spot / Jeff Szpirglas, Danielle Saint-Onge;
illustrator: Dave Whamond.
(Orca echoes)

Issued in print and electronic formats.
ISBN 978-1-4598-0791-4 (pbk.).—ISBN 978-1-4598-0792-1 (pdf).—
ISBN 978-1-4598-0793-8 (epub)

I. Whamond, Dave, illustrator II. Saint-Onge, Danielle, author
III. Title. IV. Series: Orca echoes
PS8637.Z65X2 2015   jc813'.6   C2014-906693-7
                      C2014-906694-5

First published in the United States, 2015
Library of Congress Control Number: 2014952071

Summary: Leo's penchant for exploring lands him in trouble at school until he uses his
navigation skills on the class field trip to prove he really can be responsible.

Orca Book Publishers gratefully acknowledges the support for its publishing programs
provided by the following agencies: the Government of Canada through the Canada Book Fund
and the Canada Council for the Arts, and the Province of British Columbia
through the BC Arts Council and the Book Publishing Tax Credit.

*Orca Book Publishers is dedicated to preserving the environment and
has printed this book on Forest Stewardship Council® certified paper.*

Cover artwork and interior illustrations by Dave Whamond
Author photo by Tim Basile

ORCA BOOK PUBLISHERS   ORCA BOOK PUBLISHERS
PO Box 5626, STN. B   PO Box 468
Victoria, BC Canada   Custer, WA USA
v8R 6s4   98240-0468

www.orcabook.com
Printed and bound in Canada.

18 17 16 15 • 4 3 2 1

For Léo and Ruby

Chapter One

Leo loved to explore. He had explored many places with his parents—the ocean, the mountains, even his very creepy basement!

To Leo, just walking to school each day was a chance for exploring. He liked to find different ways to get there. He would make maps of the streets to remember the way. Then, once he got to school, he would create new and interesting routes around the playground.

On Tuesday, Leo came in through the front gate and past the kindergarten playground. Then he went behind the portables, where the big kids hung out. He stopped and took out a notebook full of maps.

He had made all of them himself. Leo had just started mapping his new path when the first school bell rang.

Some of the kids started running to their classroom lines. "Hurry up," a little girl said. "We only have one minute before we are late!"

Leo put down his map. He saw a pink backpack lying beside the portable. He looked up to see Violet running to her line without her backpack. Violet's line was way over at the other end of the school. "Violet!" he called out. She did not hear him.

Leo looked to his own side of the school. The kids in his class were already lining up. Well, not lining up. It was more like a football huddle than a line. The rest of the class lines were straight as arrows. But Leo's teacher, Mr. Chang, always came to find the class jumping up and down and making gorilla noises. Eli and his friend Larry were the kings of gorilla noises. And toilet sounds.

Leo took the pink backpack and ran to Violet's line. Her class was already walking into the school. "Violet, wait! Here's your backpack."

Violet turned around and smiled at Leo. "Thanks," she said. "But now you're late for class!"

Leo turned around. At the other end of the school, Mr. Chang was already leading the class inside.

"Not again!" Leo said. "I even came early today."

Leo ran as fast as he could. He was only a few feet from the door when it closed. He pulled at the door, but it was locked. He banged on the window. Nadia, the last girl in line, looked over and saw him.

"Let me in!" Leo said through the window.

Nadia stood there for a moment and smiled. Then she stuck out her tongue at him. She turned around and followed her class inside.

Leo thunked his head against the window. "Oh, great," he said. "I have to get a late slip…again!"

Chapter Two

The only way to get back into the school was through the main doors. Leo trudged inside and went to the office. The secretary did not look up from her desk. She was busy on the phone.

"Late again?" she said.

It took Leo a moment to realize she was talking to him.

"It was not my fault," Leo said. "Violet forgot her bag."

The secretary handed Leo a late slip. "And last Friday, you tried to rescue a grasshopper from the ants."

"They were going to eat it!" Leo said.

"And the day before that, you had to help Joseph's puppy across the street."

"Right," Leo said. "He could have been hit by a car."

The secretary put the phone down. "Go to class, Leo."

She handed him a purple slip that said *LATE* in big black letters. Leo hung his head and sighed. He walked to class.

By the time he had hung up his bag, got his homework and walked to the classroom, kids were already on the carpet. Mr. Chang was sitting on his chair, pointing at two boys running around the desks. "It's circle time!" Mr. Chang said. His face was as purple as Leo's late slip.

Mr. Chang saw Leo standing at the door.

"Sorry I'm late," Leo said.

"Where were you?" Mr. Chang said.

"Violet forgot her bag," Leo said.

"I saw Leo running across the field after the bell rang," Nadia said politely. She said everything very politely. Nothing else she did was very polite.

Leo frowned.

An eraser hit the white board behind Mr. Chang. "Boys, sit down now!" he said. Larry and Eli ignored him. Mr. Chang grinned. He reached into a bag sitting by his feet. "You won't see my surprise if you're not paying attention." He pulled out a golden piece of paper from the bag. It had stars all over it.

Leo's eyes went wide. "Cool! What is that?"

"It's a special award," Mr. Chang said. "Each month I will give one away for someone who shows good skills. This month, I'm looking for responsibility."

"Responsi-*what?*" Eli asked. Then he bumped into a chair.

"Responsibility," Mr. Chang repeated. "Like coming to the carpet quietly and calmly."

Larry, Eli's friend, bumped over the same chair and fell onto Eli. "I like shiny things," Larry said.

"I could cut that up to make gold coins for my pirate treasure!" Eli shouted. Eli liked pirates a lot.

Leo stared at the shiny award in Mr. Chang's hands. His eyes went as wide as wheels. If only Mr. Chang knew how hard he was trying to be responsible each day. Like when he had saved Violet's bag.

"People who are responsible come to class on time, like Nadia," Mr. Chang said.

Leo saw that Mr. Chang was looking right at him. Leo lowered his head. He *was* responsible. Mr. Chang just never saw it.

"But enough about the award for now," Mr. Chang said, leaning forward on his chair. He tried to sound excited, even though three girls at the back were passing notes back and forth. "I have a special project to show how responsible you can be!"

Leo was the only other one leaning forward, because he saw what Mr. Chang was holding in his hand.

It was a map!

Chapter Three

Leo couldn't hold in his excitement. "What a cool map!" he shouted.

Mr. Chang stopped. "Please raise your hand if you want to share," he reminded Leo. Mr. Chang did not like shout-outs.

Leo nodded. He had to show he was responsible. He raised his hand.

Mr. Chang sighed. "Yes, Leo?"

"What a cool map!" Leo shouted.

Mr. Chang sighed again. He started to unfold a giant map, but one end flopped onto Justin's head. "Could I get some helpers?" Mr. Chang asked.

Leo raised his hand, but Mr. Chang chose Nadia and her friend Mai instead.

As the girls unfolded the map, Leo's heart raced. It was a map of the whole school. It was as long as Leo was tall. It was the biggest map he had ever seen!

"This is a blueprint of the school," Mr. Chang said. "I borrowed it from the caretakers. I told them I would be *very* responsible and take good care of it."

"Then why is Larry chewing on the corner of it?" Nadia asked.

Mr. Chang's eyebrows wrinkled. "Larry! Enough with the paper!"

"But it's *so* blue," Larry said.

"It looks like a pirate map!" Eli said. "Where's the treasure?"

Mr. Chang pulled the blueprint away from Larry. "It's not a treasure map, Eli. Look, it shows us all of the rooms in the school."

"Even the girls' bathroom!" Larry said. Then the rest of the kids started laughing.

Leo stared at the map. There were numbers on the sides that showed how large the hall was. They also showed the measurements of all the rooms in the school. He had no idea there were so many rooms. He edged closer to take a better look.

His hands fell over the map. He traced the outline of their classroom with his fingertip.

Then Leo stood up and went to his desk. He kept his map notebook inside. He pulled it out. He had already started to make his own map of the school, but he did not have enough time to visit every classroom. He could use *this* map to finish his own.

"Leo," Mr. Chang said, "it's circle time, remember?"

Leo tried to explain about his map book. "But—"

"Responsible students ask before getting up during a lesson," Nadia said quietly so that only Leo could hear.

Leo's eyes went from the map to the shining gold award.

Mr. Chang began to fold up the blueprint. "The special project is that you are going to make a map... of our classroom!"

"Wow!" Leo shouted.

"Bo-ring," said Justin.

Mr. Chang just kept talking. "We will make maps with partners. I have already chosen a partner for each of you." Mr. Chang read through the list. Leo waited and waited. Would he get stuck with Eli? Or Larry? Maybe he could work on his own.

Mr. Chang had almost gone through the whole class list when Leo heard Mr. Chang say, "Leo, you can work with Nadia. I'm sure you will both be *responsible*."

Leo's heart sank. He looked over to Nadia. She folded her arms across her chest and stuck out her tongue.

But Mr. Chang was too busy to see that.

Chapter Four

"There's just one more thing," Mr. Chang said. "It's the really special part of this project."

"Great. I bet there's a map test tomorrow," Eli huffed.

"You'll be tested," Mr. Chang said. "But not in class. We're going to use our mapping skills on a field trip in a few weeks."

"A FIELD TRIP!" twenty voices hooted at once.

Mr. Chang seemed pleased at this. He waited for the class to calm down. It took a minute or three.

"What field trip?" Justin asked. "Are we going to that stinky farm again?"

"No farms, Justin. We are going to explore the woods with an expert guide. So you need to take

15

this seriously. I'm putting twenty minutes on the clock." Mr. Chang got up from his chair and walked to his desk. There was a little clock sitting on the edge. He turned a dial on it and a little sliver of red was shown. The clock was a special timer that counted down the minutes.

Leo nodded. This was the greatest news he could have ever heard at school. A mapping field trip? In the woods? He could even bring his super-duper compass! There was just one problem...

"Oh great, I'm stuck with La-La-Land Leo," Nadia said.

Leo sighed. Nadia was not his first choice for a partner. But he knew he could map the class with his eyes closed. "Let's get started," he said.

Leo went to the front desk and got a big piece of paper. Nadia was supposed to get a pencil and ruler, but instead she went over to her friend's desk and got a colored marker. She started to draw a puppet on her hand. Leo thought about telling Mr. Chang that

Nadia was not a responsible partner. But Mr. Chang was too busy trying to unfold the paper airplane that Eli was making.

Leo looked back at Mr. Chang's timer. He tried to call Nadia over to his desk to start.

Nadia held up her colored hand and made it talk in a silly voice. "No, La-La Leo. You come over heeeeere!"

Leo shrugged. "Fine." He took the paper, went and got a pencil and ruler, then joined Nadia at her desk.

She had opened a doodle book and was using the marker to make pictures of cats. "Don't you think these are great?"

Leo stared back at the timer. "We have used up three minutes already," he said. "I bet we can get this done in *two* minutes. There's a window over there, Mr. C's desk over there. And the carpet. What else is there to map?"

Leo searched the room. He could see the whiteboard, the desks and the computer. There was also the filing cabinet with Mr. Chang's globe

on top. He laid down the paper and started to draw them out.

Nadia saw what Leo was doing and put her doodle book away. "Pencil is so boring," she said. She grabbed the paper from Leo's hand and wrote *MY MAP* on it in giant letters with her marker.

"You used up half the space!" Leo grumbled.

Nadia smiled. "It's a small classroom."

Leo could feel his face getting warm. All he wanted to do was show Mr. Chang what a great map he could make. Now the project was ruined!

He stormed away from Nadia and took the washroom pass from Mr. Chang's desk. He put it on his desk, then took another big piece of paper. First he needed a break. Then he would show Mr. Chang what he could do by himself!

Chapter Five

Leo left the classroom and headed toward the boys' washroom. A bright orange pylon blocked the way. A voice called from inside, "The washroom is closed." It was Mrs. Banks, the school caretaker. "Please use the junior washroom upstairs."

Leo's eyes went wide. The upstairs washroom? That was where the big kids went! Leo was sure he would get bonus marks for effort if he could put the upstairs washroom on his map. But could he be back in class before the timer ran out?

Leo peeked back into the classroom. Mr. Chang was busy watching the rest of the class make their maps.

And the timer still had a big slice of red on it. No problem! He would be superfast.

He took the stairs two at a time and finally made it to the second floor. His face was red and he was out of breath. But he had made it!

Leo looked all around. What a cool place! There were no coat hooks, only lockers. A few kids wandered the halls, listening to music on headphones. On one side of the hall, a display case showed shiny trophies and track-and-field medals. Leo spied a large mural covering one wall. It was painted with animals from around the world. There were zebras, hippos, owls and even a king cobra.

The primary hall only had little pictures of bunnies and some finger paintings. Sheesh. His grade really needed some better art.

Leo sat down. He added the mural and lockers to his map. He drew the cobra just the way it looked in the mural.

Bang! Leo jumped.

What was that noise? And what was that funny smell? It wasn't coming from the washroom. It came from somewhere down the hall.

Leo got up and followed the stinky smell. He found a classroom and looked through the open door.

Inside, older students were wearing goggles. At the front of the room stood a teacher in a white coat. He was holding test tubes full of bubbling blue liquid. He mixed them together. There was a puff of smoke and another loud bang. A smell like rotten eggs filled Leo's nose.

"Ewww!" a voice called out behind him.

Leo turned around. Eli was standing there.

"What are you doing here? The washroom pass is on my desk."

"It *was* on your desk," Eli said. "I got tired of waiting." He looked into the science lab. "This place is coooooool!"

Leo saw a clock on the wall. He gulped. There wasn't much time left. He began to walk back to the stairs. "Come on, Eli. Mr. Chang will wonder where we are."

But something caught Eli's eye. "Check that out!" he said and pulled Leo over to him.

Eli pointed to an art classroom across the hall. Students were sculpting large creatures out of clay. "Wow! They have a whole art room upstairs," Eli said. "I bet they don't even use crayons. Or eat them."

Then Eli stepped into the room. "Check out this bucket of clay. We could totally make pirate-ship models from that clay!"

All eyes in the room turned to Eli.

"What are you doing here?" Mr. Ross, the art teacher, asked.

"Going to the washroom," Eli said. "What does it look like?"

"It looks like you're taking our clay," Mr. Ross said. He pointed to the clock on the wall. "Shouldn't you get back to class? It's almost time for recess."

Leo dropped his things on the ground. His stomach flip-flopped. Oh no! They were going to be late! Leo picked up his things and raced back to class.

In the downstairs hall, Leo saw Nadia drinking at the fountain. Leo walked up to her. "Did you finish your map yet?" Leo asked Nadia.

"Don't you mean *our* map?" replied Nadia.

"No, I decided to make my own," said Leo.

"Leo!" a voice boomed from the classroom.

Leo turned to see Mr. Chang standing in the doorway. He did not look happy. "Where were you?"

Leo pointed to the pylon by the washroom. "I had to go upstairs," he said.

"But there is no washroom pass on your desk."

Then Eli came skipping down the hall. "Oh, hi, Mr. Chang. Look. I got us some clay!"

"Come inside," Mr. Chang said. "You have been late too many times. I hope things go better on the field trip…"

Leo's heart jumped a beat. "It's not my fault!"

But Mr. Chang had already gone back into the classroom.

How was Leo ever going to earn the responsibility award now?

Chapter Six

Over the next two weeks, Leo practiced getting to school on time every day. When recess was over, he was always the first in line when Mr. Chang came to take the students inside. "I'm front of the line again, Mr. Chang!" Leo would say.

But Mr. Chang was usually too busy helping Eli and Larry back into line to notice Leo.

Soon it was the day of the field trip.

Leo's alarm clock went off early. He bolted out of bed and raced into his parents' room. "It's the day of the field trip, Mom! You know, the one with the maps? I'm going to be responsible. Can I bring my special compass watch? It's great for mapping."

Leo's mom and dad grumbled in bed. "What time is it?"

"Five thirty in the morning! Hey, guess what? I brushed my teeth."

Leo's mom rubbed her eyes. "But your alarm clock doesn't go off for another hour."

"I set it for earlier today. See how responsible I'm being?" He beamed.

"That's great," Leo's dad said. "Why don't you go and get a bowl of cereal?"

Leo nodded. "Great idea!"

He ran out of the room.

Five minutes later there was a knock on Leo's parents' bedroom door.

"What is it?"

"Here you go!" Leo said. "I brought you breakfast in bed." He thrust two bowls of honey-coated Sugar-O's in front of their faces.

Leo smiled. Today, he was the king of responsibility!

Leo made sure he got to school extra early.

His mother pulled up to the front of the school in her car. She stared out the window. There was nobody on the playground. There were only a few cars in the parking lot.

She looked at Leo. "Are you sure you need to be here this early?"

Leo nodded. "I don't want to be late for the field trip."

"But I don't even see your teacher here yet."

Then a car pulled into the parking lot. Leo watched as Mr. Chang got out of it.

"There he is!" Leo said, pointing to him.

Leo's mom sighed. "You have a good day. Be safe!"

"I know. I will!"

Leo jumped out of the car and ran toward Mr. Chang.

Mr. Chang was carrying a stack of schoolbooks and had a big bag slung over his shoulder. He didn't

look fully awake yet. Mr. Chang tripped on a rock and dropped all of the books.

Leo sprang into action. He started helping him pick up the books.

It took Mr. Chang a second to notice what was going on.

"Leo? What are you doing here?"

"Being responsible," Leo said with a big, big smile.

Mr. Chang watched Leo pick up all of the books and stack them into a neat pile.

He took the books from Leo and gave him a long look. "Thank you, Leo. You have been very helpful lately."

"Thanks, Mr. Chang. I have been trying my best."

"I know that I have been busy with the other students. But I just want you to know how proud I am of how hard you are trying."

This made Leo's smile grow so big it filled his face.

"Do you need any more help?" Leo asked.

Mr. Chang looked past Leo. A few kids had arrived at the playground. "Is that Eli over there? It looks like he needs a buddy to play with. Why don't you play with him while I get things ready for the trip?"

"Sure thing, Mr. Chang!"

Leo couldn't believe it. Mr. Chang knew how hard he was trying. Leo couldn't wait to use his compass watch on the trip today. He could almost taste that responsibility award! And it tasted good!

Chapter Seven

Leo was so happy, he was even okay when Mr. Chang sat him on the bus next to Larry. He did not mind when Larry took the window seat and drew his name on the frosted windowpane.

Instead, Leo looked at his compass watch. An arrow on it turned as the bus moved. "What's that?" Larry asked.

"My compass watch," Leo said. "See that arrow? It always points to the north. So when I use it, I never get lost."

Larry shook his head. "But can you play video games on it?"

Leo shrugged.

Larry showed Leo his watch. There was a large screen with a video game on it. "Check it out. I'm on level twelve!"

Finally, the bus rolled to a stop at a bumpy parking spot. The doors opened and all the kids piled out.

Leo looked around. They were in the middle of a large forest. A sea of pine trees towered over them. An old cabin stood at the end of the parking lot.

The door to the cabin opened. A tall man with a red beard came out. He wore a cowboy hat and a bandanna. He also had a shiny watch on his wrist.

Larry pointed to the man. "Look at his watch! It's just like yours. No video games or anything! And check out his hat. It's supercool."

"I'm glad you like it," the man in the hat said. "It's my lucky cowboy hat. I used to be a cowboy, you know."

Then the man in the cowboy hat pulled out a whistle and blew it hard. Everybody stopped and stared at him. The man waved to the kids. "Hi, I'm Mr. Taylor. Today, you will all put your mapping skills to good use." Mr. Taylor gave the students maps of the forest.

Leo took the map. He could see all of the trail markings on it. There were red flags on the map that told you where not to go, and green flags that told you where it was safe. There were also some Xs.

Larry scratched his head. "What do those Xs mean?"

Eli came bumping up to Leo and Larry. "It's a treasure map, guys. X *always* marks the spot. But why are there so many of them? There must be tons of treasure!"

The class started to walk down one of the trails. "No, Eli. This is not a treasure map. See that red flag?" Leo said.

Eli nodded. "The red flags are where other pirates didn't find treasure."

Leo shook his head. He pointed to a tree ahead. There was a red flag hanging from a high branch. "No, that means you can't go off the path here."

Eli shrugged. "But then how do we find the treasure?"

"It's not a treasure map, Eli."

Leo walked away from Eli. He followed the rest of the class down a trail to a clearing. Mr. Taylor and Mr. Chang stopped the class.

"What are we doing now?" Leo asked.

"Now that you have seen the trail, you will explore it by yourself. Mr. Taylor and I will keep an eye on you. When you hear the whistle, come back to the clearing."

"Okay," Leo said. He started to wander off, but Mr. Chang stopped him.

"No, you need to stay with your group."

"Group?" Leo said.

"Yes. I've put you with Eli and Nadia."

Leo stopped in his tracks. He turned around. Eli and Nadia were waiting.

"Shiver me timbers, let's go find that treasure!" Eli said.

Leo groaned. This was going to be a problem.

Chapter Eight

It did not take long for Eli and Nadia to wander far away from the rest of the class and deeper into the thick woods. Leo kept looking from the map to his group. "Wait!" he said. "You took a wrong turn. Look for the green flags!"

"Green flags? Those are there to *distract* us from the treasure," Eli said.

"The red flags are prettier," Nadia said.

"No, no, no," Leo warned. "You are wandering too far away. Can't you see it on the map?"

"What map?" Nadia asked.

"The one Mr. Taylor gave us."

"The treasure map, yes."

Leo shook his head. He was supposed to show Mr. Chang how he could win that responsibility award.

Then Leo heard a loud whistle.

"Great," Leo said. "That's the signal from Mr. Taylor. We have to head back now."

"No," Eli said. "I'm going to find us the treasure. We're so close. I can feel it."

"Eli, pirates sailed boats. We are in a forest, and there is no water."

"We'll see about that. Come on, Nadia!"

Eli marched off the path and even deeper into the woods.

Nadia looked at Leo and shrugged. "Let's get him before he gets lost," she said.

Nadia followed Eli off the trail. Then Leo saw the red flag on a tree nearby. "But we're not supposed to go there!"

Leo heard the whistle blow again in the distance. And again. He could hear voices. "Leo! Nadia! Eli!" It was Mr. Chang. He sounded worried.

Leo stood there. He didn't know what to do. If he went after Nadia and Eli, they would be late getting back. And they would probably get into trouble. If he went back alone, he could say they had run off without him. He wouldn't be late, and it would not be his fault.

He heard Mr. Chang's whistle. He took a few steps back toward the clearing.

Then he stopped.

Eli and Nadia were not good with maps. It was not safe.

The whistle kept blowing.

Leo pulled out his compass watch. He looked at the needle. He knew how to get back on the trail. It was time to rescue Eli and Nadia.

He marched into the thick bushes. There were thorns that scratched at his jacket. Leo pulled his collar up so he would stay safe.

"Eli? Nadia? Where are you?"

"Oh no!" a voice called out.

Leo heard screaming and crying. He ran after the sound. Were they hurt?

"Are you okay?" Leo asked.

Leo pushed some branches aside and stopped.

Eli was standing in a mud puddle that went up to his ankles. Eli pulled his feet out, looked down at his shoes and wiped his eyes. "Look at these shoes. My mom is going to be so mad. Who would put treasure in a swamp?!"

"I don't think the Xs meant treasure," Nadia said.

Behind him, Leo could hear the whistle.

"Let's get him back, Nadia," Leo said. Together they helped Eli out of the mud. The three of them walked through the forest. It seemed bigger and darker than before.

Nadia looked around. Leo could tell she was scared. "I don't even know where we are anymore. These trees all look the same."

"Are we lost?" Eli said.

Leo looked at the map. He looked at his compass watch. He shook his head. "Don't worry. I know the way."

Leo led the group back through the forest. The sound of the whistle and Mr. Chang's voice got louder.

Soon Leo pushed the trees aside. There was the trail! He stepped back onto it.

"Leo!"

Leo turned. Mr. Chang was there. So was Mr. Taylor. So was the rest of the class.

In the crowd of people, Larry shook his head. "Wow, Leo! You are in big trouble now!"

Chapter Nine

Mr. Chang let out a big sigh. "What were you doing off the trail? We looked everywhere for you."

Leo gulped. "But…I was only trying to help…"

Then Nadia stepped forward. "He did help, Mr. Chang. In fact, he saved us."

"He did?" Mr. Chang asked.

Nadia nodded. "Eli went looking for buried treasure. I followed him. All we found were mud puddles."

Eli looked down at his shoes. "That *may* have happened."

Nadia went on. "If Leo hadn't come to get us, we would still be stuck in the mud."

Mr. Taylor and Mr. Chang looked at each other. Then they turned to Leo. "How did you know how to get back on the trail?" Mr. Taylor asked.

"Remember my compass watch?" Leo smiled. He held it up. "The needle always points north. I always know where to go when I use it."

Mr. Taylor took off his cowboy hat and put it on Leo's head. "Leo, you showed courage and responsibility. You get to wear the cowboy hat for the rest of the day."

The hat fell over Leo's eyes. "I do?"

"Yee-haw! You're the hero!"

Everybody cheered for Leo. They didn't stop cheering, even on the long bus ride back to school. Larry even let Leo take the window seat.

Leo had never smiled so hard.

By the time the bus pulled back into the school parking lot, it was almost time for the kids to go home.

Mr. Chang stood up before they could all get off the bus. "Hold up a minute," he said. "I have an important announcement to make."

Leo's classmates looked at each other. What was it?

Mr. Chang dug into the small knapsack beside him. "I'd like to announce the winner of our classroom responsibility award. He showed great responsibility not just today, but many, many days before." Then Mr. Chang pulled out the award.

All of the students leaned forward to see whose name was on it.

"Three cheers for Leo!" Mr. Chang said.

Everybody on the bus cheered. They cheered so loud that the students in school looked out the windows to see what was going on.

"Leo won the award!" Nadia screamed to her sister in the seventh grade.

Mr. Chang handed the award to Leo. "Thank you, Leo."

"Thank you, Mr. Chang." Then Leo smiled. "Mr. Chang, I have an idea. But it's a secret."

Mr. Chang leaned in close. Leo told him.

Mr. Chang nodded and smiled. "Yes, I think we should do that tomorrow."

"Do what tomorrow?" Larry asked.

Leo grinned. "You'll see."

Chapter Ten

Leo couldn't wait to show everyone the surprise. He had to keep it a secret, even when Larry and Eli walked up to him before class. "Tell us, Leo."

Leo shook his head. "You'll have to wait."

Then the bell rang. Leo went to the front of the line to meet Mr. Chang.

The class walked into the school, down the hall and to their room.

"Look at that!" Nadia said.

Taped to the door was a huge piece of brown paper with the words *TREASURE HUNT* written on it.

Mr. Chang dug into his pocket. He pulled something out and put it on his head. Then he

turned around and growled, "Arrrr, mateys!" He was wearing an eye patch.

"No way," Eli said.

"Yes way," said Leo. Then Leo opened the door and went into the room. He came out with a big stack of papers. He handed them to the rest of the students.

"Today we are going on a real treasure hunt," he said. "I made a map of the whole school. It's your job to find the treasure. Use the green flags to help you find your way." He pointed to a green flag that was on the wall in the hallway. "It's just like our trip from yesterday."

"Oh no," Eli groaned. "There better not be any mud puddles. I just got my shoes clean."

Leo laughed.

"Don't worry," Mr. Chang said. "There's no mud. But you can find the treasure if you find the X on the map."

"That's right," Leo agreed. He held up his copy of the map. "Because this time, X marks the spot!"

Leo watched as the rest of his class began hunting for the treasure. Eli and Nadia teamed up together. So did Larry and Justin. Everybody worked really hard to find it.

Of course, Leo knew what the treasure was. It was shiny and golden. It was Mr. Chang's next class award. This time, the whole class was working together to find it.

"Now *that*," Mr. Chang said softly to Leo, "is the real treasure."

Jeff Szpirglas and **Danielle Saint-Onge** are married, live together in Toronto, Ontario, and teach in classrooms with students of diverse cultural backgrounds. Jeff has written several books and enjoys writing scary novels like *Evil Eye* and *Dentures of Doom*. Danielle has a master's degree in social anthropology and is a crusader for equity in the classroom. Besides teaching, they spend their time writing stories and taking care of their twin toddlers.